Acting Edition

I0591765

Discus

by Becca Schlossberg

ISBN 978-0-573-71028-5

www.concordtheatricals.com
www.concordtheatricals.co.uk

No one shall make any changes in this title(s) for the purpose of production. No part of this book may be reproduced, stored in a retrieval system, scanned, uploaded, or transmitted in any form, by any means, now known or yet to be invented, including mechanical, electronic, digital, photocopying, recording, videotaping, or otherwise, without the prior written permission of the publisher. No one shall share this title(s), or any part of this title(s), through any social media or file hosting websites.

For all inquiries regarding motion picture, television, online/digital and other media rights, please contact Concord Theatricals Corp.

MUSIC AND THIRD-PARTY MATERIALS USE NOTE

Licensees are solely responsible for obtaining formal written permission from copyright owners to use copyrighted music and/or other copyrighted third-party materials (e.g. artworks, logos) in the performance of this play and are strongly cautioned to do so. If no such permission is obtained by the licensee, then the licensee must use only original music and materials that the licensee owns and controls. Licensees are solely responsible and liable for clearances of all third-party copyrighted materials, including without limitation music, and shall indemnify the copyright owners of the play(s) and their licensing agent, Concord Theatricals Corp., against any costs, expenses, losses and liabilities arising from the use of such copyrighted third-party materials by licensees. For music, please contact the appropriate music licensing authority in your territory for the rights to any incidental music.

IMPORTANT BILLING AND CREDIT REQUIREMENTS

If you have obtained performance rights to this title, please refer to your licensing agreement for important billing and credit requirements.

DISCUS was first produced by the Hunger & Thirst Theatre in The Jeffrey and Paula Gural Theatre at the A.R.T./NY Theatre Spaces in March 2022. The performance was directed by Jenn Susi, with costumes by Christopher Metzger, lighting design by Austin Boyle and Paige Sebel, and sound design by Randall Benichak. Technical supervision by Patrick T. Horn. Stage management by Alyssa Rios. The cast was as follows:

ZEPHYRUS..................................... Alejandra Venancio

NOTOS ....Rita McCann

BOREAS .... Alexander Settineri

APOLLO .... Philip Estrera

ARTEMIS ....Patricia Lynn

HADES...................................... Victoria M. Fragnito

HYACINTH/GANYMEDE ....Patrick T. Horn

CHARACTERS

M – Male, **F** = Female, **NB** = Nonbinary

GF – Genderfluid (meaning, you can cast an actor of any gender in this role)

TITANS

ZEPHYRUS – god of the western wind (F or NB)

NOTOS – god of the southern wind, sister to Zephyrus (gender fluid)

BOREAS – god of the northern wind, sister to Zephyrus (gender fluid)

OLYMPIANS

APOLLO – god of music and poetry and healing and many other things (M)

ARTEMIS – god of the hunt, Apollo's twin sister (F or NB)

HADES – god of the underworld (gender fluid)

MORTALS:

HYACINTH – a Spartan prince (M), doubles as **GANYMEDE**, a mortal servant of the gods

SETTING

The space in between life and death and many other locations in ancient Greece.

AUTHOR'S NOTES

This isn't the ancient Greece you know; anything can happen here.

When we think of ancient Greece, we usually think of cis white men or cis white women. The casting should work against this as much as possible. Theatres should use best efforts to ensure that BIPOC actors make up at least 50% of their casts and that one actor is trans and/or nonbinary. Diverse casting should be especially apparent in the families. If a sibling is cast with a white actor, at least one of their siblings should be played by an actor of color.

Pronunciation

Deady: like daddy, but "dead," instead of dad

Gaia: guy – ah

Tartarus: tar – tar – us

Orion: oh – rye – uhn

Therapon: thera – pawn

Hephaestus: huh – fay – stuhs

Philtatos: Phil – tah – tohs

A few more quick notes

Pace should be lightning fast, except when its not.

I would highly recommend intimacy choreography and a pre-show intimacy call. Safety and comfort for the actors is key.

If the expletives won't work for your production, you may remove them/amend them. They are there for emphasis and to heighten intensity.

I owe a great debt of gratitude to Patricia Lynn, who served as this play's dramaturg, producer, and original Artemis. I would ask that she be credited in your program as such.

α. (One)

(A Runway.)

(A spotlight on the discus, center.)

(HYACINTH *enters, violently, as if shoved into the space.)*

(HYACINTH *sees the discus.)*

HYACINTH. Oh shit, am I dead?

(Studies the discus.)

Where am I?

What happened...

How did I...

Apollo?

Apollo? Can you hear me?

I will pray to you. Apollo.

How do I pray again...?

Right! I bend at the knees.

(HYACINTH *kneels, turns his palms upward to face the heavens.)*

I hold out my hands

And I speak to you

And the words will turn into birds

And these birds will reach you

HYACINTH. They will whisper in your ear

You'll tell me what happened.

Tell me why I'm here.

Apollo...

I'm scared.

Can you hear me?

> (**APOLLO** *enters on the opposite side of the runway.*)

Apollo. It begins with you.

> (*Transition rapidly into.*)

β. (Two)

(A "Benefit for Mortals" banner is flown.)

(The party where **HYACINTH** *and* **APOLLO** *meet.)*

APOLLO. Welcome, welcome, welcome, gods and humans alike, for the one and only Benefit for Mortals! I am your host for the evening, Apollo, but maybe you know me better as the Great God Apollo (am I right, am I right.)

Well, you know, it is such an honor to be hosting this event – a night to ensure all mortals have a permanent home on Gaia. More than ever, it seems our human brethren are being threatened by the gods – volcanoes, earthquakes, war, famine! But fear not, the Benefit for Mortals was founded to ensure that all gods come together in solidarity to protect and preserve this incredible population. To show support, we have prepared a lineup of gods and beauties that are going to light up this rock! Let's kick off this treasure trove, shall we?

*(***ARTEMIS*** enters, walks the runway.)*

Great-goddess-of-the-hunt, it's my own twin sister, Artemis, looking very stylish indeed. Could we talk to you for just a quick moment?

(She ignores him, exits.)

Really in a hurry, I guess. Anyway, who's that coming next down the line?

...

...

Um...

APOLLO. Must be a bit of lag...

Over two hundred gods and goddesses were invited tonight so...some of them are bound to show up.

(**ZEPHYRUS**, **NOTOS**, *and* **BOREAS** *enter, walk the runway.*)

Oh, what heavenly winds are approaching! Blowing into view: Selene's daughters, the three winds: Zephyrus, Boreas, and Notos. Let's see if we can...Ladies, a quick word? Can you say a word to all the mortals watching?

BOREAS. Umm...

NOTOS. We're very happy to be here.

APOLLO. And Zephyrus, what would you say to all the mortals out there?

ZEPHYRUS. Just that I'm such a fan. I think one of the things that speaks to me most about humans is their vulnerability.

APOLLO. Totally.

ZEPHYRUS. They really depend on us and we really depend on them.

APOLLO. Totally, absolutely.

ZEPHYRUS. I guess that's why I am so disheartened to see the mortals still putting their faith in the Olympians.

APOLLO. ...what's that?

ZEPHYRUS. Well, here you have these mortal beings, just, praying to the gods that have raped and pillaged them for centuries. If the Titans had control –

APOLLO. Excuse us.

(**APOLLO** *as gracefully as he can, leads a protesting* **ZEPHYRUS** *off stage, leaving* **NOTOS** *and* **BOREAS** *in the spotlight. As he is doing so:*)

NOTOS. ... *(Motions for* **BOREAS** *to say something.)*

BOREAS. Hiii morts! Love you!

(Rapid transition:)

γ. (Three)

(Inside the Benefit.)

(The gods drink, isolated in their own circles.)

BOREAS. This Benefit for Mortals really blows.

NOTOS. Tell me about it.

BOREAS. The guest list is just so tame this year.

NOTOS. Remember last year? Hades was here?

BOREAS. Uggggh, Hades.

NOTOS. Poseidon.

BOREAS. Oh, love me a fish god.

NOTOS. He could have left Medusa in her cage, but at least he bothered to show up.

BOREAS. The popularity of the mortals is really shifting amongst the gods.

NOTOS. Oh, they're falling out of favor, no doubt, no doubt, like, Prometheus didn't even come! The god that sculpted the mortals out of clay doesn't even show up at the ceremony to benefit them! Like, here, I'll just create the problem, and then slither back to my little hole in Gaia. It won't be long before his little experiment over-populates and destroys the earth all together.

BOREAS. I hear that.

NOTOS. You'd think Zeus would show up. Apollo's like, his favorite.

BOREAS. Zeus has no favorites. And he's here, trust me, he's probably just disguised, as a fucking swan or something.

NOTOS. Do you think Apollo hosted just to get more prayers?

BOREAS. Who knows why he did it, although...you know what they say about a Benefit for Mortals?

NOTOS. What?

BOREAS. Do you really need me to tell you?

NOTOS. No. I just want the conversation to stop.

BOREAS. It's just a big ole orgy for the gods to feast on the mortals naïve enough to show up.

NOTOS. Mm, consuming them for their own perverse pleasure.

BOREAS. They keep this up, they'll be a bunch of half-breed mutants on the planet.

NOTOS. Or something equally perverse.

BOREAS. How about you, Zeph?

NOTOS. Yeah. You gonna snag yourself a little deady to play with?

ZEPHYRUS. A what?

NOTOS. A deady. A mortal.

BOREAS. Who's your deady?

(**ZEPHYRUS** *moves to exit.*)

NOTOS. *(To* **ZEPHYRUS**.*)* Where are you going?

ZEPHYRUS. *(Exiting.)* To get air.

NOTOS. She is air. She's the western wind.

BOREAS. Maybe she's off to the dessert buffet?

NOTOS. You mean that pocket of mortals gathered in the back?

BOREAS. Okay, hey, I know I said all those nasty things, but it doesn't mean I won't sleep with one. Or twenty.

>   (**BOREAS** *and* **NOTOS** *look in opposite directions at their prospects, then back at each other.* **BOREAS** *then forcefully takes* **NOTOS**' *hand and they exit together.*)
>
>   *(Transition to:)*

δ. (Four)

(**ZEPHYRUS** *finds* **HYACINTH** *on a balcony.*)

(**HYACINTH** *is engaged, acting out an imaginary discus throw.* **ZEPHYRUS** *startles him.*)

HYACINTH. Oh, thank gods, it's just you.

ZEPHYRUS. *(Pun intended here.)* Hiya.

HYACINTH. Hello, hello, look what luck has blown my way. You know how I hate these things.

ZEPHYRUS. You're not alone. If another god brushes their hand over my skirt and calls me "outspoken," I'm going to lose my shit.

HYACINTH. Sorry about that.

ZEPHYRUS. You're the only one and it is so appreciated.

HYACINTH. And a deady at that.

ZEPHYRUS. Please don't do that.

HYACINTH. Who's your deady, Z?

ZEPHYRUS. No, you are an idiot, but...you are in no way my deady.

HYACINTH. I kinda am, though...

ZEPHYRUS. Please stop talking.

HYACINTH. It's okay. I know you'd rather be out here with me than rolling with the rest of them.

ZEPHYRUS. I want to crush them with stones. Or melt them. Or decapitate them. But don't worry, I'd make sure you were not around.

HYACINTH. Because I'm special?

ZEPHYRUS. Mortal. And kind...too kind for these parts. Why even have benefits, who are they benefiting? And why are you hiding out here on the balcony?

HYACINTH. Training.

ZEPHYRUS. Training for what?

HYACINTH. For Apollo's games.

ZEPHYRUS. ...Et tu?

HYACINTH. He's starting a huge competition in Delphi and Sparta will take the gold.

ZEPHYRUS. Surely you're joking.

HYACINTH. Spartans don't have a sense of humor.

ZEPHYRUS. You want to play in that one's puffy shadow?

HYACINTH. He's the best. Playing in that shadow would probably make anyone, at least, better.

ZEPHYRUS. Apollo is like...don't mean to bust your bubble here, but he's like, horrible. Just...horrible. Pompous. Arrogant. And like...the phoniest of all the Olympians.

HYACINTH. Oh, something just hit me.

ZEPHYRUS. What?

HYACINTH. Some gossip, it...it seems to radiate from you.

ZEPHYRUS. Uh huh.

HYACINTH. I hear rumors fly on the wind.

ZEPHYRUS. Yes, and crash into people's ears when they're not listening.

HYACINTH. Ever play a part in that?

ZEPHYRUS. Can you even get that thing up into the air?

HYACINTH. What?

ZEPHYRUS. The discus...can you even get that thing up into the air?

HYACINTH. That's why you train.

ZEPHYRUS. I can help you train.

HYACINTH. You can?

ZEPHYRUS. Don't act so surprised. One blow from my winds and I'll have that thing right up in the air.

HYACINTH. *(Smiles.)* ...You're certainly a wind who knows what they're doing.

ZEPHYRUS. Well without my winds, you couldn't even play your little game. And neither could any Olympian. Are you aware of that?

HYACINTH. I am.

ZEPHYRUS. Care to see it in action?

HYACINTH. We shouldn't leave the benefit, right...?

ZEPHYRUS. Oh, come on. You're the one hiding out here on the balcony. I'll take you into the sky. You liked that.

HYACINTH. ...I want to meet every cloud...

ZEPHYRUS. So, come meet them, sweet prince.

(He takes her hand and they exit.)

(Transition rapidly inside to.)

ε. (Five)

(**APOLLO** *and* **ARTEMIS**.)

APOLLO. I told them a million times. Call it the Benefit for Humanity! Calling it the Benefit for Mortals sounds like they will only be here until the end of the week! Which is the opposite point of this entire evening! This is what happens though when these demi-idiots don't listen to me.

ARTEMIS. Yes, I'm sure you think the name was the problem with this evening.

APOLLO. Is there anything you care to address, sister?

ARTEMIS. Excuse me?

APOLLO. Quite the runway entrance.

ARTEMIS. I don't have to talk at these things, Apollo. You're lucky I bothered to show up.

APOLLO. And I feel so lucky.

ARTEMIS. Our blessed father didn't show up tonight. No gods from the other realms.

APOLLO. Well, I imagine they are all engaged.

ARTEMIS. Apollo. Come on. They don't care. They care more about brandishing their armor than the fate of these mortals. And the only reason you care is because… I don't know? You're low on their prayers and you need them to jerk you off for a little while?

APOLLO. …I get plenty of prayers. In fact, I can hear those little birdies' wings fluttering right now. I appreciate you coming, sister.

ARTEMIS. Where are you going?

APOLLO. I should catch up on some of those prayers. Last time I checked, I had too many to count. *(Taking keys out of his pocket.)* Might as well do that in my chariot.

ARTEMIS. You're leaving your own party?

> (**APOLLO** *exits.*)

> (**ARTEMIS** *takes a shot.*)

> (**ZEPHYRUS** *re-enters, a moment as she tries to make herself more presentable, (post-sky sex).*)

Zephyrus.

ZEPHYRUS. Artemis.

ARTEMIS. Would you care to join me?

ZEPHYRUS. I'd be curious why.

ARTEMIS. You look like you could use a drink.

> (*Hesitantly,* **ZEPHYRUS** *approaches* **ARTEMIS'** *table.*)

> (**ARTEMIS** *lays out the shots and they toast awkwardly and drink.*)

How are your plans to burn down Olympus going?

ZEPHYRUS. Why? Care to join in?

ARTEMIS. You really seem to hate my brother. I do find that incredibly attractive.

ZEPHYRUS. Well, fire should rain down upon his head. Or hail. Fire hail.

ARTEMIS. You've already had a drink or two, I see.

ZEPHYRUS. You want tips on bringing your brother down, Artemis? Because why else is this happening right now? Oh. Oh, wait.

ARTEMIS. What?

ZEPHYRUS. I see...this is because of Orion, isn't it?

ARTEMIS. ...

> (**ARTEMIS** *takes a shot.*)

ZEPHYRUS. You really are thinking about it, aren't you? Joining the other side? Make sense, you're one of the few Olympians that spends more time on earth than up here on the mountain. In those great forests of yours. You should remember, that earth you're running on, that was made by Titans.

ARTEMIS. Maybe I just care about my brother suffering...

ZEPHYRUS. And you should, huntress of the hunters, because he is a plague on Gaia. Hope you enjoy the rest of this Olympian party, Artemis. And I am sorry for your loss.

> (*Transition to:*)

ς'. (Six)

(Another balcony. **APOLLO** *is on the way to his chariot.* **HYACINTH** *is alone, practicing again.* **APOLLO** *goes unnoticed for a moment and watches.)*

APOLLO. Too much movement.

HYACINTH. *(Star struck; dead.)*

APOLLO. You need to plant your feet. The power of the throw comes from how well you're grounded.

HYACINTH. ...Yeah. Sorry. Or should I say...apologies. Get it? Apollo-GEEZ *(Hates himself.)*

APOLLO. Not a worry. That tip was for free.

HYACINTH. Thank you.

APOLLO. Let's see it.

HYACINTH. *(Nervous.)* Sure. Yeah. Whatever.

(**HYACINTH** *does a slightly better throw.)*

APOLLO. Better! That would land in Troy.

HYACINTH. Wouldn't make it past the Aegean Sea. You're just being kind.

APOLLO. I'm not though. I'm not kind.

HYACINTH. But you are known for...kindness that you bring to people.

APOLLO. Well...

HYACINTH. You hosted this benefit...

APOLLO. Not to worry you, but...they were a bit desperate for a host. I wouldn't call me kind just yet. And it seemed to suck this year, so, I don't know. What'd you think of the benefit?

HYACINTH. Oh no, I thought it was great. Yeah. I love these things.

APOLLO. Do you?

HYACINTH. ...I don't. I'm just desperately afraid of saying otherwise.

APOLLO. Oh, I love it when humans lie in this way. The looks on your faces. It's too good.

HYACINTH. Glad you enjoy it.

APOLLO. I do. Your first lie to me then. I will treasure it.

(*Beat.* **HYACINTH** *to* **APOLLO.**)

(**APOLLO** *back to* **HYACINTH.**)

Would you like to know a secret?

HYACINTH. Yes. Yes.

APOLLO. I hate these things too.

HYACINTH. You do not.

APOLLO. I do.

HYACINTH. But you're known for these parties.

APOLLO. They serve a purpose. But. I wish they were more for the causes themselves rather than for the gods filling their egos. But I'm no better. Truth is, as popular as I am, I loathe responsibility. But Duty...she does call.

HYACINTH. Yes, she does.

APOLLO. And you were sent to represent Sparta?

HYACINTH. You know who I am?

APOLLO. I've heard tell of a handsome Spartan prince. I'm told he would be entering my games come summer.

HYACINTH. (*Nervously chuckles.*) ...Cool, yeah...that... that's awesome, but...but now, I'm really done for because...well, as you can see, I'm not very good.

APOLLO. Oh no, don't be so hard on yourself. There's great potential there.

HYACINTH. If you say so…

APOLLO. I do. And my words are prophetic, so.

HYACINTH. …Then I'll keep at it.

APOLLO. Good. Perhaps…another tip?

> (*He gestures for* **HYACINTH** *to once again demonstrate his throw.*)

> (*A moment as* **HYACINTH** *nervously stands in front of* **APOLLO**.)

Throw for me.

Go slowly. Very slowly.

> (*Beat.*)

HYACINTH. Yeah…sure…

> (**HYACINTH** *throws in slow motion.*)

APOLLO. Okay, freeze.

> (**HYACINTH** *freezes.* **APOLLO** *approaches him, but does not make physical contact.*)

First. And this is crucial. Clear your mind. Nothing quite so detrimental to humans than their pesky thoughts. Take a big breath. Then release it.

> (**HYACINTH** *drops the position, takes a big breath and releases.*)

Good. Relaxation. Quite key. Then it's fun, right?

HYACINTH. (*Laughs, maybe nervously.*) Sure. Fun. Less fun is building enough muscle to throw the discus.

APOLLO. Yes. There's that.

HYACINTH. I wonder where I could get training like that.

APOLLO. Well, you should only get it from the best. And by best, it's me.

HYACINTH. I have seen you throw before.

APOLLO. In which competition?

HYACINTH. No. Alone, actually. In the stadium in Delphi. I hope you'll forgive me for spying a bit. But. It's the Great God Apollo, what else could a mortal do, you know? You threw, and...it rocketed past Selene and headed straight to the Beyond. Unreal. You weren't sweating. You didn't bat an eye. And then...

APOLLO. What?

HYACINTH. Something else when your arm fell. The look on your face.

APOLLO. Exuberance?

HYACINTH. Sadness. A great sadness I have never seen on a god.

APOLLO. ...

HYACINTH. Forgive me, I don't mean to –

APOLLO. Forgiven. There is a loneliness in godliness. Most mortals don't see that, but it's true. I do, I wish sometimes I could be, just...

HYACINTH. Human?

APOLLO. Human? No. No, no, no, no. No. No. The sky. Or the clouds. Something without form. Human?

HYACINTH. *(Bristling.)* Didn't mean to offend.

APOLLO. No, sorry, I just...I envy not, what you...what you will...

HYACINTH. What we will become? There's a loneliness in that, too.

(**ZEPHYRUS** *enters. She can sense the sexual tension between* **APOLLO** *and* **HYACINTH** *right away.*)

Zeph. You must know...

ZEPHYRUS. Apollo. Great God of Music. Of Poetry. Of Justice. Of Order. Of Reason. Of Prophecy. Of Healing. Of Disease. Archery? Did I leave anything out, or is that your full resume?

APOLLO. Well, without my temples and accolades, it does feel a bit scant.

ZEPHYRUS. Not enough time then.

APOLLO. *(To* **HYACINTH**.*)* We know each other, yes. Great speech before on the runway.

ZEPHYRUS. Oh, thanks, I like to keep things interesting.

APOLLO. If only the Olympians took you seriously, think how interesting things would become. It's a shame they don't. How are things in the West? Still windy? Cause that's what you're the goddess of, right? Wind? And that's it?

HYACINTH. Excuse me, I'm going to get a drink before they shut down the party.

(**HYACINTH** *exits.*)

ZEPHYRUS. Now look what you did.

APOLLO. I was about to say the same.

ZEPHYRUS. Unbelievable.

APOLLO. Is it? Or is it reason? He favors me. You can see it plainly.

ZEPHYRUS. Fuck your reason, Apollo! He has been favoring me every day for the past season.

APOLLO. Well, a new season has arrived.

ZEPHYRUS. I know being an Olympian makes you believe you are entitled to whatever it is your little heart desires, but he's not yours. You don't own him.

APOLLO. Nor do you, Titan.

(**BOREAS** *enters, wasted.*)

BOREAS. Zeph, Zeph, have you tried the wine? Between me and Notos, I don't think these mortals are prepared for like, the shit storm of a wind-nado that's coming tonight. (*A beat, observing.*) What's up with you?

ZEPHYRUS. Apollo and I were just chatting.

BOREAS. Uh...been there, done that.

(**BOREAS** *kind of wanders drunkenly around.*)

APOLLO. I feel strongly about this one.

ZEPHYRUS. You feel strongly. Well, how exciting for you that must be.

BOREAS. Zeph. Zeph. Do you know where the loo is? Never mind, I will just find it myself. Excoose.

(**BOREAS** *stumbles to the exit.*)

APOLLO. Zephyrus, I'd prefer to keep this civil, but if you insist, I want to draw your attention to one thing: do you know why you can come to my parties and say your little words and live your little days without interruption?

ZEPHYRUS. Because I'm the daughter of a Titan? And we are not so easily moved?

APOLLO. Because I let you. Because we, these Olympians you hate, let you.

ZEPHYRUS. You let me? Oh! So, I should be thanking you then?

APOLLO. Because in the end we know, it's not worth starting a war over a Titan goddess. But now I'm thinking, maybe in all that kindness, in all that turning a blind eye, maybe you're forgetting who you are and who I am, so, let me remind me you: don't forget who you are and who I am. The cost will be too great.

ZEPHYRUS. You will never let me forget.

APOLLO. Is it war you want?

ZEPHYRUS. War. Cause you're good at that, right? You know a thing or two about war, Apollo. And how to wipe out generations of men.

APOLLO. Leave it, Zephyrus.

ZEPHYRUS. You will do absolutely anything to have your way.

APOLLO. No, I'm just good at playing the game, Zephyrus. Sorry for that.

ZEPHYRUS. What game is that exactly? The game of murder? Your sister told me moons ago. She told everyone, really. Everyone knows what you did to that poor mortal she dared to love. You knew that, didn't you? That she loved him. And yet, you destroyed him. As you have destroyed so much. For so many. For so long. And that's not even...one page of that resume. What right do you have to love at all?

(**NOTOS** *enters.*)

NOTOS. Zephyrus, let's float. This benefit is on its last leg, no offense, Apollo.

(**HYACINTH** *enters.*)

ZEPHYRUS. Did you get your drink?

HYACINTH. Yeah.

ZEPHYRUS. Are you leaving?

HYACINTH. I was actually going to hang back. If that's okay.

ZEPHYRUS. Of course.

> *(She touches his cheek.)*

> *(The action stops. The lights shift. Transition to:)*

> *(**HYACINTH** pulls away, frightened, into darkness.)*

HYACINTH. What was I doing?

I was praying...

Why was I praying?

Oh yeah, to know...to...

> *(**HYACINTH** lowers to prayer position.)*

Apollo?

Can you hear my prayer?

Apollo?

Please...What's happening to me?

> *(We hear **APOLLO**'s voice.)*

APOLLO. *(Voice over.)* Hyacinth.

I'm here.

I can fix it.

I can fix it. Just. Just hold on. Please.

I'm here.

> *(**HYACINTH** touches his hand to his heart.)*

HYACINTH. *(Continued.)* Apollo...

There's a...scary, sick feeling...

It's underneath my ribs.

I needed more force.

I'm not...I wasn't planting my feet...

I didn't

Extend...?

What is happening to me?

> *(He practices his throw. Stylized. A haunted movement.)*

> *(**APOLLO** is behind him now.)*

ζ. (Seven)

(They are practicing together on a sunny day.)

APOLLO. Excellent! Well done.

HYACINTH. Yeah?

APOLLO. Yes. That was it. That was the umph.

HYACINTH. One more!

APOLLO. He does not tire.

HYACINTH. Is it bad?

APOLLO. No. It's what I like about you.

*(**HYACINTH** throws again.)*

Impressive! You have come so far.

HYACINTH. Still a long way to go.

APOLLO. Hyacinth.

HYACINTH. Yeah?

APOLLO. You're doing it again.

HYACINTH. Listen. I'm a prince. People placate me a lot.

APOLLO. Well, I am not. I see you. I see all the effort you're putting in. You are remarkable. Very different than any human I have ever met. And all this...

HYACINTH. Yeah?

APOLLO. It just makes me happy. Watching you.

HYACINTH. That makes me happy, too, Apollo. You have no idea.

APOLLO. I have some idea.

HYACINTH. No one has ever seen me like this before.

APOLLO. I've been around awhile, you know? It takes a wonder such as you to knock a god like me off their mantle.

HYACINTH. I still need to throw a discus that weighs fifty obols.

APOLLO. And you will! There's a reason that it is further along in the competition.

HYACINTH. It's easy for some.

APOLLO. Well, they can't all be as good me. Where would the fun be in that?

HYACINTH. You go now.

APOLLO. Again?

HYACINTH. I like watching you. It inspires me.

APOLLO. If I must.

HYACINTH. You must.

> (**APOLLO** *goes to the fifty-obol-discus and picks up with ease. He throws it perfectly down the runway and offstage it goes.*)

Clear into the stands. Nothing slowing it down! Incredible!

APOLLO. Yes, I know.

> (**HYACINTH** *sits, tired and in awe.*)

Tired, finally?

HYACINTH. Yeah, I'm about done.

APOLLO. Nothing left in you?

HYACINTH. Not really, no.

> (**APOLLO** *tickles him, starts to playfully fight him.*)

HYACINTH. Don't start with me! I will call the Spartan army upon you!

APOLLO. They couldn't take me.

HYACINTH. No. They couldn't.

> *(It devolves into a hitting match with a few stray slaps lingering. They may kiss and kiss.)*

APOLLO. Suddenly, he has all this energy again.

HYACINTH. I have a good teacher. He taught me...stamina.

APOLLO. Ridiculous human.

HYACINTH. Do you think I can keep up with this pace through the spring?

APOLLO. With some rest, I do.

HYACINTH. It'll be better in the spring. I can't wait. The flowers will be back then.

APOLLO. ...I have no idea how to respond to that.

HYACINTH. Come on.

APOLLO. You realize you're a Spartan, right?

HYACINTH. And you're the god of music! You don't feel anything when you look at beautiful flowers?

APOLLO. I suppose I do, but it's just...

HYACINTH. What?

APOLLO. It's just so sweet.

HYACINTH. Come on...

APOLLO. Too sweet. Sweet Prince Hyacinth and his sweet, sweet flowers.

HYACINTH. You're teasing me.

APOLLO. I'm not. I'm sorry, I'm not.

HYACINTH. Flowers give people hope, you know? Gods must know how much hope means to us.

APOLLO. Hope is what keeps us employed.

HYACINTH. Can I ask you for something then? Directly?

APOLLO. Ask me for what?

HYACINTH. Can you leave the ones that grow in front of the stadium? It always looks so bleak when they hack them all down before the games. Trying to look all masculine, woof; it looks barren and desolate.

APOLLO. Hyacinth, it's too much.

HYACINTH. Come on.

APOLLO. I am overwhelmed by the sweetness.

HYACINTH. This isn't teasing?

APOLLO. No. I don't mean it to be.

HYACINTH. Can you? Please. Don't make me pray to you. Just, tell me to my face?

APOLLO. Of course. Yes. This is a very easy thing I can do for you.

(**HYACINTH** *falls into him with gratitude.*)

HYACINTH. Flowers will give the athletes a good boost, you'll see.

(**HYACINTH** *swats at the air by his ears.*)

APOLLO. Hey, what's wrong?

HYACINTH. Rumors. Those wind sisters, they...they do know how to spread them.

APOLLO. I'll say another enchantment.

(**APOLLO** *rises, raises his hands and begins to mumble prayers in a circle around them.*)

HYACINTH. I should get used to it. I suppose. You don't mind it?

APOLLO. I'm used to being on people's lips. It's not a terrible place to be. Good or bad.

HYACINTH. A lot of people seem to be really upset or jealous.

APOLLO. We're the scandal of Olympus, pal.

HYACINTH. Why?

APOLLO. Why? You tell me. What are they saying?

HYACINTH. That I'm mortal. Your first mortal.

APOLLO. Boring.

HYACINTH. That I'm...male. And that figures. Because your only interest is pleasure.

APOLLO. And I'm a narcissist. And I'm arrogant. They'll say things until they have run out of breath, and still, I am one of the most popular gods in Olympus. Put it out of mind, Hyacinth.

HYACINTH. That I am your favorite...

APOLLO. What? Prince of princes?

HYACINTH. Toy.

APOLLO. Toy? Who says that?

HYACINTH. The whole of Olympus. Your little...deady.

APOLLO. Well. They don't know you. And they don't know me. And that's Olympus.

HYACINTH. Yeah.

APOLLO. It's exhausting, but.

HYACINTH. Yeah...

APOLLO. Try and put it out of mind.

HYACINTH. I'll try.

APOLLO. I'm making it stronger.

HYACINTH. No, leave it, Apollo, it...it doesn't matter. It's unavoidable.

> (**HYACINTH** *puts a hand on his shoulder.* **APOLLO** *softens, finishes the prayer.*)

Perhaps I should go home to Father. Gods know it, but he'll probably have a wife waiting for me when I return.

APOLLO. Must avoid those at all costs.

HYACINTH. Maybe the rumors would ease if I were to return, but. I want to train. I want to train here with you.

APOLLO. And you are brave for doing so.

HYACINTH. Well, they're wrong. All of them. You treat me like an athlete. An equal.

APOLLO. I am glad you are here.

HYACINTH. Me too. And...as your equal...

APOLLO. ...Yes?

HYACINTH. I should ask you for something. Something to seal this in truth. Something of consequence.

APOLLO. More flowers?

HYACINTH. ...No, like...your declaration of love? For example?

APOLLO. ...My declaration of...?

HYACINTH. Apollo?

APOLLO. Sorry, uh...I guess that word makes me nervous.

HYACINTH. I thought gods didn't get nervous. Isn't love something gods just know?

APOLLO. Gods don't know love...any more than humans do.

HYACINTH. Sure seems like *you* do. You're the god of music. Seems like you get it all.

APOLLO. Love is not something one "gets." Always tested. Always rough. Always…a consciousness.

HYACINTH. A consciousness?

APOLLO. A cycle of consciousness.

HYACINTH. Apollo. Come on, you're talking about love like it's a science. Have you really never known a love before?

APOLLO. Well, the only experience I've had with it, it was not of my own will. Eros poisoned me with it, but it was not real. In my experience, it always ends. And usually badly. How do you endure it when it always ends?

HYACINTH. Gods can endure anything, Apollo. You probably shouldn't ask me how one endures.

APOLLO. How do mortals?

HYACINTH. Endure love? We accept it…and love anyway. It changes, but. You have to accept that change. It can grow or it can fade. But it starts with acknowledgement.

APOLLO. …

HYACINTH. So, please, do keep me posted on how you're feeling.

APOLLO. …You're disappointed.

HYACINTH. I'm here…

APOLLO. Or we could make you immortal and then problem solved.

HYACINTH. I never thought the god Apollo would be afraid of anything.

APOLLO. I'm not afraid. I'm a problem solver. I mean, think about it. Talk about a love that will endure.

HYACINTH. Then it is true what they think. I am only your equal if I am also a god.

APOLLO. Oh, forget what they think. You are my equal now. But you could be forever.

HYACINTH. Maybe you should use that old prophecy thing of yours to find out how you'll feel?

APOLLO. ...I already have.

HYACINTH. And?

APOLLO. It's incomplete. Even for me. I see only the present, the rest is...

HYACINTH. The rest is?

APOLLO. Nothing.

HYACINTH. No, come on. The rest is?

APOLLO. No, that. It's nothing. Nothing. I see only... shadows.

HYACINTH. ...You see only shadows?

APOLLO. I wouldn't worry. When it comes to matters of the self, even the gods can be blinded...even I cannot see my own fate.

HYACINTH. ...I think I do need some rest.

APOLLO. Will you come here?

> (**APOLLO** *is sitting by then.* **HYACINTH** *rests his head on him.*)
>
> (*The light shifts.*)
>
> (*A moment. Almost in slow-motion, as...*)
>
> (**HYACINTH** *rises, steps out of the tableau.*)

HYACINTH. You never said it, did you?

HYACINTH. I can't remember.

I feel like there is so much I can't remember now.

Apollo? Please.

What am I trying to remember?

> (**HYACINTH** *turns to run but he comes face to face with* **ZEPHYRUS.**)

> *(He inhales sharply.)*

> *(Transition to:)*

η. (Eight)

ZEPHYRUS. Oh, hey stranger.

HYACINTH. Hey.

ZEPHYRUS. Where ya been?

HYACINTH. Training.

ZEPHYRUS. Training. Ah. No wonder you look a fright.

HYACINTH. I'm on a break – I only have a little bit of time.

ZEPHYRUS. Yeah. The life of an Olympian. Always sweating. Always running around on the ground. Everything I hate, really.

HYACINTH. I know.

ZEPHYRUS. You're training with Apollo?

HYACINTH. I know you hate that, too.

ZEPHYRUS. How's it going?

HYACINTH. It's going good.

ZEPHYRUS. Yeah. Is it fun?

HYACINTH. It can be.

ZEPHYRUS. Are the rumors true?

HYACINTH. Which ones?

ZEPHYRUS. Because I've heard you're doing more than just training.

HYACINTH. ...That one's true.

ZEPHYRUS. That you're both exclusive now or...?

HYACINTH. I don't...I mean...

ZEPHYRUS. And please don't tell me you're his therapon, or, companion, or whatever the term is, because I am so sick of hearing that bullshit about men in Greece.

HYACINTH. I wouldn't put it quite like that.

ZEPHYRUS. I haven't seen you. At all.

HYACINTH. That actually has more to do with the training, than...

ZEPHYRUS. Uh huh.

HYACINTH. But it has to do with Apollo, too.

ZEPHYRUS. Because he has you.

HYACINTH. No. What? No. I have him.

ZEPHYRUS. ...I see...

HYACINTH. For now, anyway. I'm sorry, Z.

ZEPHYRUS. It's fine. But for your sake, I think it might be best to tell you the full truth about this god that you are allegedly keeping.

HYACINTH. What do you mean?

ZEPHYRUS. I mean, I wonder how much you've heard. About him. About his past.

HYACINTH. He's immortal? His past encompasses a millennium.

ZEPHYRUS. And?

HYACINTH. Zeph, look, maybe you're confusing him with some of the other Olympians you hate, and I get that, but...Apollo's the god of music. He's known for his brilliance.

ZEPHYRUS. Oh, Hyacinth...

HYACINTH. What, "Oh, Hyacinth?"

ZEPHYRUS. How have your own people not...spoken of it? But, no, I guess that is what a generation removed will do to a people. And they wanted to forget. What he did to the people of Greece. To the Spartans. To your own people. During the Trojan War. Do you know how Troy came to hold advantage over them? A deadly plague. Sent by none other than the God of Disease himself. The kind of plague that turns a society into chaos. The kind that rips open the flesh, turns men into balls of pus. That releases such human suffering you could not believe. And death only made him stronger. After that, the people of Greece, they cowered to him. His popularity soared. After that, he never stopped killing. Even recently...his sister's lover. Orion. A mortal. And he murdered him for virtually no reason at all.

HYACINTH. ...

ZEPHYRUS. Believe it. Because every word of it is true. He masquerades as a god who loves mortals, who would throw benefits for them, host parties and games, but he only wants what he can take. And I bet...I bet he's never said a word to you about any of this, has he?

HYACINTH. ...Well...

...I don't care.

ZEPHYRUS. ...What do you mean *you don't care*?

HYACINTH. He's not like that with me.

ZEPHYRUS. Are you fucking insane?

HYACINTH. Why are you doing this, Z?

ZEPHYRUS. Why am I –? Did you hear what I just said?

HYACINTH. Fine, but why are you doing this, Z? Why are you –

ZEPHYRUS.	HYACINTH.
Look –	Just because what we had has ended –

ZEPHYRUS. Oh, so, it *is* over?

HYACINTH. Didn't you know it would only make me hate you?

ZEPHYRUS. Gods should protect people! Not conquer them. Not harm them. That is our duty! That's what we are supposed to give. How can you not see he's ensnared you? It's all part of his ploy for power. He's only taken you to get what he wants! And you...I care for you. It's harsh but I did it to protect you.

HYACINTH. Protect me? Z...

...I love him.

...I love him. There's no protecting me now...

ZEPHYRUS. With this knowledge, you can protect yourself, you idiot! Or do you really want to be another mortal lost to the clutches of the gods?

HYACINTH. I want to stay. I want to stay with him. Stay with the god I know.

ZEPHYRUS. Hyacinth –

HYACINTH. I must. And our love will keep growing. It will erase all that came before.

ZEPHYRUS. You cannot erase a monster. Sooner or later, you will get hurt.

    (**HYACINTH** *turns away from her.*)

    (*The lights shift.*)

    (**ZEPHYRUS** *lingers, perhaps, staring hard at his back.*)

HYACINTH. What was I doing?

I need to pray.

    (*He kneels, outstretches his hands.*)

Where am I?

I'm remembering something

I'm remembering

How awful some memories are

How they make you cringe

Apollo. Help me.

I'm still alive.

> (*If* **ZEPHYRUS** *is still there, she exits.
> Transition:*)

> (*A burst of energy:* **APOLLO** *enters, running,
> tossing his body playfully into* **HYACINTH**'s,
> *and a chase begins.*)

> (**HYACINTH**, *forgetting himself again, is lost,
> swept away in it, trying to outrun* **APOLLO**.)

θ. (Nine)

HYACINTH. Come on, almost at the top!

> (**HYACINTH** *beats him to the top. Looks out at the view.*)

APOLLO. Incredible.

HYACINTH. What?

APOLLO. You're so fast. Too fast!

HYACINTH. Not as fast as you.

> (**APOLLO** *sits by* **HYACINTH**. *They look out together.*)

It's beautiful.

APOLLO. And look: beautiful view of the jasmines. Crocuses over there...

HYACINTH. ...Did you learn the names of the flowers?

APOLLO. Violets...and those...those are pink irises.

HYACINTH. Slain. I'm dead.

APOLLO. Good. That was the intent.

HYACINTH. I can see Helios in his chariot.

APOLLO. Incredible, right? Nothing matches it. Except mine. We will have to ride in it one of these days. My father gave it to me when I was born: six giant swans driving a golden base. It's...Next Level.

HYACINTH. I'd love that.

APOLLO. I should have taken you already. But. I will not be able to keep the enchantment up there.

HYACINTH. Right.

APOLLO. And all will see us.

HYACINTH. Who cares? If they must think of me as Apollo's favorite accessory, then, so be it. Maybe that will finally make the rumors stop.

APOLLO. Not just any accessory, but my favorite one.

HYACINTH. Right, right...Because I am not that? Right?

APOLLO. I'm joking. Of course not.

HYACINTH. We both know...I am more than a toy, I am a being, a being that's...entitled to know things of importance.

APOLLO. Yes...Of course.

HYACINTH. Are there any things of importance you care to share with me?

APOLLO. Like what? Hyacinth, what's happening right now...If you want to ask something, just ask me.

HYACINTH. Zephyrus.

APOLLO. ...That's not a question.

HYACINTH. She told me. She told me, you've done terrible things...Before me. Is it true?

APOLLO. ...There's a reason they say the Western wind is a jealous wind.

HYACINTH. But is it true?

APOLLO. Listen, have I asked you for anything? Other than, you know, an extra push-up here and there?

HYACINTH. No.

APOLLO. Have I been unkind?

HYACINTH. Answer me, Apollo.

APOLLO. Have I though? Am I unkind?

HYACINTH. It is unkind to be dishonest. You have to be honest, Apollo. You have to show yourself in love or the love is...it's not true. Be honest about your past. Or have you not even dared to face it?

APOLLO. You said you wanted nothing from me but flowers and my love. Is that true?

HYACINTH. That's not what I'm talking about, Apollo.

APOLLO. Can you just give me now? I just, I...I have wrestled with this and I cannot speak for the lifetimes before you. But I can ask that you give me now. And...I will do the same. And that's it, right?

HYACINTH. How long have you been planning to say that to me?

APOLLO. ...What?

HYACINTH. How long?

APOLLO. I don't know.

HYACINTH. Sure you do.

APOLLO. ...the night after I met you.

HYACINTH. ...You lied.

APOLLO. Omitted.

HYACINTH. I wish I could see it as plainly on your face as you can on mine.

APOLLO. It's the product of a few lifetimes.

HYACINTH. What have you done?

APOLLO. Is there nothing you hide from me?

HYACINTH. No! There is not. I am altogether sweet and boring!

APOLLO. I wanted to start again. I felt anew. You showed me it could be different, I could be different.

HYACINTH. But it is not different. Because you lied.

APOLLO. I didn't want to tell you because I knew this would happen! I knew you would hate me in the end. And now, you do!

HYACINTH. That sounds as though you're blaming me.

APOLLO. You – you are too good, for me, Hyacinth, that is the truth of it. You are sweet, and you are innocent, and you aren't meant to be with me.

HYACINTH. No, no no no, you don't get to do that!

APOLLO. Do what?

HYACINTH. Disappear behind a trap you laid! You did this! This was not me, or who I am, or what I am. You did this! And now you must reckon with it. I'm going back down.

APOLLO. I could make you immortal!

HYACINTH. ...What?

APOLLO. I know a flower. Across the sea. That, and a lift of my hands, and then, you'd be one of us. And you would see, endless time... There are so many versions of yourself you leave behind.

HYACINTH. Is this what you were expecting to happen? To freeze me in time so you could keep me like this forever?

APOLLO. This is the greatest gift I can give you!

HYACINTH. Honesty would have been better.

APOLLO. It is for your sake. Not mine.

HYACINTH. Immortality's not in the cards for me, Apollo.

APOLLO. Why? *Why?* I don't understand. Why would you subject yourself to the torture of a human death if you don't have to?

HYACINTH. Because I'm human, Apollo!

Because this is the way I'm supposed to be.

I'm going back down.

(**HYACINTH** *walks away from* **APOLLO.**)

(*The lights shift.*)

(*As* **ZEPHYRUS** *enters.*)

(*Sees* **APOLLO.**)

(*And we transition to:*)

ı. (Ten)

(The stadium.)

ZEPHYRUS. Hello, Apollo.

HYACINTH. ...What is this?

ZEPHYRUS. Are the rumors true?

HYACINTH. I don't remember this.

ZEPHYRUS. I'd like to see him, please.

HYACINTH. I think my mind is really going...

APOLLO. He's resting. And unable to take visitors.

HYACINTH. This cannot be my vision.

ZEPHYRUS. Is he? I heard you're not delivering him his messages.

APOLLO. Says who?

HYACINTH. Apollo, are you showing me this?

ZEPHYRUS. My sisters. The people. I've heard his father wants him back and you're keeping him prisoner here.

HYACINTH. You must be showing me this.

APOLLO. There are no chains on him, Zephyrus.

HYACINTH. You're here, aren't you? You're keeping me alive...so...your memories are blending into mine.

APOLLO. Nothing's keeping him here but his own free will. Perhaps that's why it's so maddening to you.

ZEPHYRUS. No, the people are fueled by jealousy. But I'm not jealous, Apollo, that's not why I'm here.

APOLLO. Sure.

ZEPHYRUS. That would be easier for you, if I were jealous.

APOLLO. Easier?

ZEPHYRUS. No. Unlike you, I genuinely care for mortals, and I fear for this one in your hands.

APOLLO. You fear for him?

ZEPHYRUS. Yes. Now that he knows the truth, he couldn't possibly want to stay.

APOLLO. You speak for him now, too?

ZEPHYRUS. I'll speak *to* him. Tell him I'm on his side. Then I'll blow back to the West, and you will never hear so much as a whisper from me again.

APOLLO. ...Zephyrus, I know the Olympians and Titans have never been able to share this world –

ZEPHYRUS. Because you stole it out from under us.

APOLLO. My father stole it.

ZEPHYRUS. And you HELPED him by murdering the Titans of Delphi ALL BY YOURSELF!

APOLLO. Be that as it may, who made you my jury?

ZEPHYRUS. Does being the god of justice exempt you from justice, Apollo?

APOLLO. ...I need not justify myself to you, no matter how tempting.

ZEPHYRUS. You need not justify yourself to anyone, if no one holds you accountable.

APOLLO. I need not justify myself to you because you are...

ZEPHYRUS. Yes?

APOLLO. Not worth it! Maybe that's why he hasn't seen you? Have you even considered that? Good effort, Zephyrus. You tried your best. But the best god won, that's all!

ZEPHYRUS. And there it is. The pompous arrogance of entitlement! And the one who calls himself the god of justice. What kind of terrible universe would allow you to call yourself by such a title? Only a universe that must be broken down and rebuilt, piece by piece –

APOLLO. This is your final warning, Zephyrus.

ZEPHYRUS. In whatever way we can. Until you have nothing!

> (**ZEPHYRUS** *lifts her hand, to cast her powers on* **APOLLO**.)
>
> (*But,* **APOLLO**, *seeing this, gets the jump on her, and casts his hands over* **ZEPHYRUS**.)
>
> (*She cowers in pain.*)

How are you doing that??!

APOLLO. You forget, transfiguration is also one of my many gifts. I'm about to turn the Western wind into the toad she is.

ZEPHYRUS. You – you wouldn't –

APOLLO. Just listen.

> (*He holds it.*)

I call myself the god of justice because I can take justice when I see it fit. The price I pay for it is something you cannot see because I will never show it to you. But you will never be my judge. So. I'd suggest you get the hell out of my stadium and leave Hyacinth to make his own decisions.

> (*He releases his hold.*)
>
> (*A moment as she recovers.*)
>
> (*Then he exits.*)
>
> (**ZEPHYRUS**, *a moment as she pulls herself together. Then:*)

ZEPHYRUS. You will win a battle or two. But in the end, the sins of your past will find you. Even the strongest god cannot stop the storm.

(**ZEPHYRUS** *rises, exits.*)

(**HYACINTH** *watches her go.*)

(*Transition to:*)

ια. (Eleven)

HYACINTH. It was you...

It was a beautiful day.

It was...beautiful that day. Helios was out in full.

We were both upset. Angry. Tired. We thought

We'd play a quick round, it would cheer us up, we said.

And.

He told me to run.

I was running so fast, trying to forgive him

trying to outrun it all

he sees me and, I know he only wants what's best, and

why is love so hard

running so fast, I could feel him smiling at it, I could feel his pride running along with me...

And he threw...

(**APOLLO** *enters. Throws the discus. Stylized.*)

I was just ahead of it. I pulled out from under it. As I turned, I saw in the back of my eye, a change in the discus.

A violent change that no natural wind could be responsible for...

Coming from the West...and...sailing it, careening it back towards...

Me.

Right towards –

Me.

I saw it coming towards me.

HYACINTH. It's a discus, I thought.

A circle...

Like me now...

Like what I'll become...

Not yet...

Not yet...

Not until I ask you

I have to ask you.

Zephyrus...

> (**HYACINTH** *kneels to pray, outstretches his hands.*)

I pray to you now...

I will speak to you and the words will turn into birds

And the birds will reach you

And they will ask

What good did it do you?

Why did you get to decide?

Why didn't I have a say?

Do you feel better?

Why did you take it all from me?

I was just beginning...

There was no chance

no chance...to feel anger.

I feel it now...

It...

Pulses

And it...

Bares its teeth...

And you would leave me like this?

Someone who I once called a friend...?

Hear me call out to you now.

Tell me the answers

Face me

or with every bit of energy I have left, I will haunt you

I will haunt you until my soul is finally at rest

>   (**HYACINTH** *quietly exits.*)

>   (*The sound of birds taking flight. A haunting reverb follows it.*)

>   (**HADES** *enters with* **APOLLO** *on the far side of the runway.*)

>   (*Transition to:*)

ιβ. (Twelve)

(**HYACINTH**'s *bedside.*)

(**APOLLO** *kneels by a thin, marble altar, caring for a body we can't see. Or, if there is an actor here, their face should be covered for the rest of the play.*)

APOLLO. Hades. You're here?

HADES. Alright, kid, where is it?

APOLLO. Where is...?

HADES. Don't play dumb, Apollo. His soul. Where is it? Let's take a look at the numbers today, okay? (*Consulting their list.*) I got one, two, seven thousand forty-three souls in attendance. 'Cept one! This one. Right there! Okay. A Spartan. With hardly any face left.

APOLLO. His name is Hyacinth.

HADES. Whatever.

APOLLO. You don't...you don't have his soul?

HADES. No! Why do you think I would have traveled up from Tartarus? To sunbathe? To look at your pretty face?

APOLLO. Oh, praise be...it means its working...it means... he's still alive.

HADES. Yes. Good. We're caught up. This is exactly what I came here to talk to you about, Apollo.

APOLLO. There will be no talking. I'm not giving you his soul. I intend to make him better.

HADES. Make this...? Kid. Have you cracked?

APOLLO. I have a plan!

HADES. I'm not interested in your plan, Apollo. Whatever it is keeping his soul from me is rooted in whatever it is you're doing to his body there. So do right by me and undo it. Now. I shouldn't have to ask twice. And after the journey I had to make to get all the way up here! The layovers I had to endure! So, let's not waste any more of my time.

APOLLO. I can fix him, Hades. Please. Please I just need... A mighty ingredient. I know such things exist.

HADES. You know, do you?

APOLLO. Like a few drops of the River Styx. The river that runs through the land of the dead. Just a few drops.

HADES. Uh huh...

APOLLO. For instance...

HADES. Oh, Apollo. Apollo, Apollo, Apollo, I've always treated you nicely, you know? You're like a nephew to me. Sort of. But now, you're really pissing me off.

APOLLO. With your help, my plan will work.

HADES. Why on Gaia's green earth would I do that? Give you some drops of the River Styx. First of all, like I just *carry* samples of the River Styx with me? Like I'm some kind of *idiot* messenger god like Hermes? I'm a businesswoman*, Apollo. I'm more careful than that. I came here to get his soul from you, not to open negotiations.

APOLLO. But the circumstances are unique! You could make an exception.

HADES. Do I look like a god who makes exceptions? If a mortal is lost in the Nether Place, I take that very seriously.

APOLLO. The Nether Place?

---

* *You can change this to fit the actor playing* **HADES**

HADES. Aka the *Loser* Place. The bane of my existence. Whatever fuckery you're doing to his body, it's not saving him – his soul is stuck in a dimension in between life and Tartarus. So, the kindest thing you can do for him is to cut him loose. Help him get back to where he belongs.

APOLLO. Yeah, in Tartarus, of course. With you.

HADES. It is his sad, mortal destiny.

APOLLO. I'll repair the body so his soul can return to this plane.

HADES. Okay, I see we are not getting very far here, so, let's just go with your plan for a second, okay, I'll play teacher here, if I must, even though that is abhorrent to me, but if only to show you the glorious faults in your thinking. Say, I give you a few drops, which I would never do, but let's say, I do, and your magic worked. And his body is restored. And his spirit, somehow, finds its way back. After a separation like this, and the damage that's been done here, his spirit will never be the same. When their soul is flung from the body like this...there is no coming back to what was. And nothing will change that fact. Not the River Styx. Or Zeus' lightning. What's gone, is gone.

APOLLO. You can't be –

HADES. I am certain. It is the nature of my business. It's what keeps me employed. But. This doesn't mean we can't do some negotiating though. Something that will help both you and him find peace.

APOLLO. What?

HADES. You don't want his soul with me? Fine. I'll keep it far from me. I'll put his soul in the sky...a constellation consolation.

APOLLO. No. I can heal him. I can heal him on my own without any of you.

HADES. Yeah, good luck with that.

APOLLO. You'll see. You'll all see.

HADES. We'll see? Kids. Egos as big as their chariots. I mean, sure, I control the fabric of the mortal universe and, you, what do you control again? You have to learn the hard way, I guess.

APOLLO. I'm the god of healing.

HADES. And the god of disease.

APOLLO. None of you know what I'm capable of. But you'll find out soon enough.

HADES. Sure, sure, sure. You heal him then, god of healing. And when it fails, call me. *(Leaves their card on the bedside.)* Here's my direct line, I am available twenty-four/seven/three hundred and sixty-five. I don't take breaks. I don't take vacations. And I'm sure after your plan fails, I'll be in a much kinder place to start negotiations.

APOLLO. ...

HADES. I'll get his soul. Eventually, they always end up with me, kid. That's just how it goes.

> *(**HADES** exits.)*

APOLLO. *(To **HYACINTH**.)* Don't listen to her*. There are so many things I can try.

Hyacinth. Are you here with me?

Hyacinth...

> *(Then, **ZEPHYRUS** enters, breathless.)*

> *(She stumbles to the ground, rests her weary body on it.)*

** Again, you can change this to fit the actor playing **HADES***

ZEPHYRUS. Hyacinth...

      (**APOLLO** *exits.* **NOTOS** *and* **BOREAS** *enter.*)

      (Transition to:)

ιγ. (Thirteen)

(The home of the wind sisters.)

NOTOS. Is it true then?

BOREAS. Is it?

NOTOS. Did you?

BOREAS. Yeah, did you?

ZEPHYRUS. Did I, what?

NOTOS. Did you strike down that poor mortal with a discus?

BOREAS. Yeah, with a discus?

NOTOS. Cause it was like their favorite thing, right?

ZEPHYRUS. What does it matter to you both?

NOTOS. Wow, okay.

BOREAS. She totally did.

ZEPHYRUS. Can you both just leave it?

NOTOS. They have been driving you insane and now...

BOREAS. Now you put an end to all that.

NOTOS. Honestly, this is the most exciting thing you have done in ages. You struck a blow to the Great God Apollo. You ruined his favorite thing!

BOREAS. The Titans are like, so excited. Oceanus, Phoebe, all the rest, they are even talking of war!

NOTOS. A war. No way!

BOREAS. A holy war between Titans and Olympians! This is only the beginning. Think of all the other damage we could do if the Titans unleashed their true powers.

NOTOS. Although. The Olympians will retaliate. Apollo will surely retaliate when he comes to.

BOREAS. Yeah Z, he is going to end your days.

NOTOS. Maybe that will like...only further the war effort?

BOREAS. But that's all only if he dies. It really hinges on that. I hear the mortal lives. For now.

NOTOS. He lives?

BOREAS. Yeah.

NOTOS. No! Oh, Z. Oh, no...

ZEPHYRUS. He...

NOTOS. You didn't know?

BOREAS. Oh, Z, you didn't know that you didn't kill him totally?

ZEPHYRUS. ...

NOTOS. So, what, he's just like, fatally wounded?

BOREAS. Facially wounded.

NOTOS. What?

BOREAS. When Z hit him in the face she like, erased his face. He has like, no face anymore.

NOTOS. I heard he has bulging bloodshot eyes.

BOREAS. I heard he has no eyes at all.

NOTOS. I heard his blood oozed out of his crown in giant puddles. They say even with fresh grass in the stadium, there will always be a stain.

BOREAS. I'm pretty sure he has no eyes, and no face, and if he doesn't have a face anymore, how can he live? Mortals can't live without faces, right? That's what I don't get.

NOTOS. It's like that one time Hephaestus roasted those mortals that dare set foot on his mountain, so he melted the skin right off their bones by making the mountain erupt with his great, gorgeous fire.

BOREAS. Right.

NOTOS. But I guess it's not like this, because none of those mortals lived.

BOREAS. Mm.

NOTOS. Went to the great beyond to do nothing, but sit and fester away as souls without the pleasure of their bodies, in a true meaningless existence, forever and always. Ugh, disgusting.

(*The sisters finally take a breath.*)

Well, sister? Nothing to say about it?

ZEPHYRUS. ...

NOTOS. Zeph, you could be the leader the Titans have been seeking. Whatever it is you're thinking, don't look back now!

BOREAS. That mortal probably deserved it, right? They always do. I'm sure whatever you did, it was for a just cause, right, sister?

ZEPHYRUS. ...

NOTOS. Anyway, we'll leave you to your thoughts, I guess.

BOREAS. Notos and I can't stop talking about you. You know how our words can travel.

NOTOS. It's only of a matter time before we are restored!

BOREAS. So proud of you!

ZEPHYRUS. You're...?

BOREAS. Sure. That Olympian pig finally got what was coming to him.

(They exit.)

*(**ZEPHYRUS** breathes.)*

(A long moment of being alone. Something is unsettled in her.)

ZEPHYRUS. It's okay. It had to be done. I had to do it.

(Once again, The sound of birds in flight. Frantic wings. A haunting echo.)

*(**ZEPHYRUS** rises, frightened, holding her head.)*

ZEPHYRUS. Please stop praying to me.

*(**NOTOS** and **BOREAS** enter again to pass through the room.)*

NOTOS. Are you sure you're okay, sister?

(She storms past them.)

ZEPHYRUS. Move!

(Transition rapidly to:)

ιδ. (Fourteen)

(**HYACINTH**'s *bedside.*)

(**APOLLO** *kneeling.*)

(**ARTEMIS** *enters.*)

ARTEMIS. Apollo? How long has it been like this?

APOLLO. ...

ARTEMIS. You cancelled the games?

APOLLO. ...

ARTEMIS. The people said you were still here. With him. Where it happened. But...I didn't believe them.

APOLLO. ...

ARTEMIS. So many days have passed...

APOLLO. ...

ARTEMIS. I didn't think you would still be here.

APOLLO. ...

ARTEMIS. The mortals think you've become a recluse in your own stadium. Haunting it like a lost soul...

APOLLO. I don't care...

ARTEMIS. They say you're doing things to the body. Dressing him. Holding him. Even though the body has already started to smell...

(**ARTEMIS** *gets a better look at* **HYACINTH.**)

APOLLO. ...He's still alive...

ARTEMIS. He looks poisoned. Like he's...like he's...

APOLLO. (*Puts his hands to his cover face to keep himself from breaking.*) ...

ARTEMIS. His face...

APOLLO. Please, don't...

ARTEMIS. I fucking hate mortals.

APOLLO. ...I hate them, too.

ARTEMIS. Don't agree.

APOLLO. I do, though.

ARTEMIS. Don't agree. Shut up.

APOLLO. ...

ARTEMIS. I'm sorry... I can't stay here in this. This is unbearable...

APOLLO. Do you think he's beyond saving?

ARTEMIS. What?

APOLLO. You are a great healer, too, Artie. Do you, do you think he is beyond saving?

ARTEMIS. Even if I thought otherwise, why would I tell you that?

APOLLO. Because you wouldn't let this mortal die, even to spite me... You care too much.

ARTEMIS. Do you know what he really looks like right now, Apollo? He looks like how Orion looked at the end. Gray. Cold. But, oh no, you...you weren't there for that part. You just...struck him down and then left. Why was that, again?

APOLLO. He...

ARTEMIS. Yes? Please, go on. Please.

APOLLO. He was an imbecile...

ARTEMIS. And who gave you such authority to decide? To rob me of my love? I am happy this is happening to you. I'm so fucking happy I hate myself for it!

APOLLO. Artie, please, PLEASE –

ARTEMIS. Please, WHAT?

APOLLO. ...I cannot take it back, Artie.

ARTEMIS. DON'T you...HOW DARE YOU –!!

APOLLO. I would if I could!

ARTEMIS. You're missing a key phrase in there Apollo. It's "I'm sorry." But you're not really sorry, are you? Just sorry that your actions have made it so that I won't help you now!

APOLLO. I am sorry, Artemis! You're my twin! Don't you think I miss you? I did it to protect you and, I – I was wrong. Entirely! I DO wish I could take it back. Regardless of now. Regardless of this!

ARTEMIS. ...It's too late, Apollo. And now another mortal dies at our deceit.

(**ARTEMIS** *moves to the exit.*)

APOLLO. Artemis, please! PLEASE! For Orion! You'll honor him!!! I know you're better than me, okay? Then all of this!

ARTEMIS. Then change it, Apollo! Change it! You are one of the few on top who can! Greedy, reckless Olympians, fix it yourself!

APOLLO. You are an Olympian, too.

ARTEMIS. Yeah, I wish I wasn't! I wish I had never seen the disgusting Mountain! Gaia is the best thing to come out of this universe and our father conquers her and curses her with blood. This home, this place I love so much. But. Neither of us will be in his grasp much longer.

APOLLO. What does that mean?

ARTEMIS. It means I leave the mountain. I'm going to live on earth.

APOLLO. You said that before. A millennia ago. Father will summon you back.

ARTEMIS. He'll be too busy. The Titans are calling for war. When your mortal dies, it will be the sign the Titans are waiting for.

APOLLO. War?

ARTEMIS. And maybe this time they will have the aid of Apollo's twin sister.

APOLLO. You wouldn't –

ARTEMIS. I suppose this is farewell then.

APOLLO. You'd join them? Just for spite?

ARTEMIS. I'd join them because it's time for a change. You've all held the keys for too long and look what you've wrought. With Hyacinth's death, it will be unwritten.

APOLLO. Artemis, he is innocent! It is my sins you see, and you are right, but...he did nothing to deserve such hell. All of us have lost sight of what is important. Please help me fix him. We can right this wrong and spare further bloodshed.

ARTEMIS. ...He's beyond saving, Apollo. He's done.

     *(**ARTEMIS** exits.)*

     (Transition to.)

ιε. (Fifteen)

(A Titan party.)

(The wind goddesses stand together.)

(The sound of birds wings, frantic flight, is heard.)

(**ZEPHYRUS** *is the only one who seems to notice.)*

NOTOS. You were surprisingly short on the runway.

BOREAS. Yeah, you barely said three words during your interview.

NOTOS. Care to comment?

BOREAS. She's not gonna comment to you. If she was, she'd have done it outside.

NOTOS. Way to inspire the troops, Z.

BOREAS. Yeah, whatever hope we had of rallying the rest of the Titans is dwindling by the minute.

NOTOS. Well, that sneaky little human hasn't died yet.

BOREAS. That thing still isn't dead?

NOTOS. You know he's not dead! Do you see anyone here celebrating? The Titans keep waiting and waiting, but as the days pass, that little deady keeps on *not* being dead!

BOREAS. All our dreams snuffed. Figures.

NOTOS. In many ways, Z, you've only caused further disappointment.

BOREAS. Agreed! And what's worse is that you won't even offer an opinion one way or the other!

NOTOS. You do realize we are the source of gossip in this world and we can't even get a word from the source!

BOREAS. Take a side, why don't you?

(The sound of birds' wings is heard again in increasing intensity.)

NOTOS. I can't take this. We have to talk about something else.

BOREAS. Well, I did hear –

NOTOS. Oh good, tell me! Tell me anything. Anything to stop talking about this festering disappointment!

BOREAS. Well, Hera and Ares are still in that net!

NOTOS. Shut up!

BOREAS. Like. I guess like, when you cheat on your husband with the god of war, make sure your husband's not a disfigured, metal-works genius?

NOTOS. Can you imagine being married to that creature?

BOREAS. Can you imagine him trapping you in a net for days on end to like, publicly humiliate you?

NOTOS. Oh, oh OH! I do have one little piece of deliciousness. Speaking of public humiliation...

BOREAS. Oh, so, this is –

NOTOS. Yes.

BOREAS. Tell me.

NOTOS. Selene is having her little mortal lover cast in the sky.

BOREAS. Shut UP!

NOTOS. I'm serious!

BOREAS. *Mom!*

NOTOS. She like, couldn't take it when he got old, so, she's having Zeus take his nooks and crannies and turning him –

BOREAS. Ew, so gross, nooks and crannies!

NOTOS. And having him turned into stars and put in the sky!

BOREAS. Like, I'm sorry. What is the big deal when she knew he would die anyway?

NOTOS. Such overkill.

BOREAS. So stupid...

NOTOS. They're mortal. They're supposed to die. Isn't that right, Z?

BOREAS. She said, isn't that right, Z?

ZEPHYRUS. I need to leave.

BOREAS. Leave?

ZEPHYRUS. Yeah. Right now.

NOTOS. Fine. Go then. We're not leaving.

ZEPHYRUS. Oh sure. I'm sure you'll want to keep up the gossip all night. Enjoy that.

BOREAS.	**NOTOS.**
...	...

ZEPHYRUS. And for the record, I think it might behoove both of you to *do* something for once in your miserable lives rather than just *talk* about the things others are doing. See what that's like.

> (*As* **ZEPHYRUS** *tries to leave, the sharp sound of a bird's cry stops her in her tracks.*)

NOTOS. Oh, like, half-murder mortals, like you?

BOREAS. Don't, sister.

NOTOS. What? Is that what you mean? What do you want us to do? What is it do you think you've done?

BOREAS. Yeah, you know what, Zeph, it's not like you killed Apollo or anything.

NOTOS. I mean, everyone knows you can't do that.

BOREAS. So, you wounded his pride, Big Whoop.

NOTOS. You caused a little stir.

BOREAS. It was a real whopper, your fifteen minutes.

NOTOS. I mean, the only spicy thing about this, is that you claimed to love these mortals so much.

BOREAS. But then you still ended up using one to hurt a god.

NOTOS. For your own ego, really, apparently, not for anyone else's!

BOREAS. I mean, that's poetic. That's riveting. Apollo will rebound. But you...

NOTOS. You will forever be tainted by this act.

BOREAS. Which will no doubt, in time, only be reduced to an act of jealousy.

NOTOS. After all, he was your deady, this mortal, wasn't he?

BOREAS. So you got jealous.

NOTOS. And wanted to steal him back.

BOREAS. But it was useless. Just like you.

NOTOS. So, I guess, you're really just like all the rest of us, aren't you, Z?

BOREAS. Not even you can claim to be different.

> (**ZEPHYRUS** *tries to exit in the other direction, but again the sound of the birds' frantic wings stop her where she is.*)

NOTOS. Dude, she is fully having a meltdown right now.

> (**ZEPHYRUS** *doesn't respond, she just stands there channeling energy.*)

And what is UP with all the birds?

BOREAS. Oh, I know what it is! Her prayers are trying to reach her, but she won't let them in.

NOTOS. Who's even sending you prayers right now?

BOREAS. Good point. Who would pray to such a loser goddess?

NOTOS. Z, what are you doing?

BOREAS. Z, calm down, don't –

> (*A burst of ferocious wind explodes out of* **ZEPHYRUS**. *It sends the party into chaos. The winds sisters are forced to take cover and we hear the sounds of glass shattering and panicked screams.*)

> (*Transition rapidly to:*)

ιζ. (Sixteen)

(Far away and outside. A little while later.)

*(**ZEPHYRUS**, enters, still stormy, frantic, breathless. She paces. Thinks maybe she is okay for a moment.)*

(Then, the sound of the birds wings in flight, approaching.)

ZEPHYRUS. No no. You can't –

Stop it, stop! SHUT UP!

(Another.)

Leave me alone!

(And another.)

Please! I didn't know!!! Hyacinth, please...please. I made a mistake. It was a mistake!

(The birds stop for a moment.)

I'll tell you.

(A moment of nothing. Then:)

I didn't plan it.

I saw his happy face. I saw the discus. I wanted to turn it on him. But I don't, because...I cannot destroy him. It's true. I know my own strength. But then I see you. Your mortal body...and I finally know the way to bring him down.

You were aligned with him! You do not care, well, some of us can get away with not caring!

I wanted to show him. I wanted to hurt him as he hurt me. As he hurt everyone around him!

But not you.

It shouldn't have been...Not you.

I floated away through his screams...his terrible screams, knowing...knowing somehow you aren't dead.

I would ask for your forgiveness

But I don't feel you would grant it.

Hyacinth, would you grant it?

> *(After a moment.)*

> *(A flutter of wings, and **ZEPHYRUS** is struck with a new loneliness.)*

Hyacinth?

Hyacinth?

> *(Transition rapidly to:)*

ιζ. (Seventeen)

(**HYACINTH**'s *bedside*.)

APOLLO. Hyacinth. Stay with me. Please. Please just hold on.

(**GANYMEDE** *enters, disheveled, from a long journey*.)

GANYMEDE. Great God.

APOLLO. Who are you?

GANYMEDE. Ganymede, great one. Zeus has sent me.

APOLLO. Zeus? Did Artemis tell him I was here?

GANYMEDE. No, he – Zeus, he – sorry, out of breath. Never been a messenger before. Usually I just...pour wine. Yikes. There were a lot of stairs. He sent me of his own accord.

APOLLO. ...

GANYMEDE. Is something wrong?

APOLLO. No, you – I haven't seen anyone. In many days.

GANYMEDE. I should have been here sooner, but I was behind schedule, a little bit. Sorry about that. It took me awhile to get the items he asked me to bring, but. I got 'em! I got them both.

(**APOLLO** *take the items*.)

APOLLO. Ambrosia...and nectar...how? How did you get these?

GANYMEDE. Quite the odyssey, I can assure you, but bottom line: Zeus told me to. So. I could not fail.

APOLLO. But. Why?

GANYMEDE. Why?

APOLLO. Why would he do this? No Olympian wants me to succeed.

GANYMEDE. No, he does! He totally does. Sorry, I'm not – maybe I'm not delivering the message right. He values me...very much...to send me here with these items, it is of great importance to him.

APOLLO. What did you say your name was again?

GANYMEDE. Ganymede, great one.

APOLLO. Servant of the gods. Yes. He abducted you and took you to Olympus.

GANYMEDE. That – I mean – He – well, I mean...

APOLLO. ...

GANYMEDE. I mean, I guess you're right, he didn't really ask me or my father nicely before he took me. But. Apparently, it's a real honor, so.

APOLLO. You are mortal.

GANYMEDE. I am.

APOLLO. At first, I thought by the glow of you, you were a god.

GANYMEDE. I get that a lot. That's why your father said he abducted me in the first – anyway! Anyway! That's not important. Look at me, rambling on! I just needed to reach you and...to bring the items.

APOLLO. You could have run off.

GANYMEDE. I would never do that. No. I'm honored to serve the gods. It's an honor!

APOLLO. Bullshit. I bet you want the Olympians torn to bits, don't you?

GANYMEDE. What? No.

APOLLO. How could you not? Why would he send you to me?

GANYMEDE. To serve you!

APOLLO. To help me get over it, right?

GANYMEDE. ...He may have mentioned that.

APOLLO. Uh huh.

GANYMEDE. But I'm not supposed to tell you that. Shit. Sorry. I'm really not a good messenger.

APOLLO. He does love his tricks. And to pass his mortal servants around like a pox.

GANYMEDE. I think he hoped with me you'd be consoled? And I'm not...I know I'm not a god, or, an athlete, even, but...

APOLLO. Or of your own free will.

GANYMEDE. Still. I could be of use to you.

APOLLO. You should not be of use to anyone. You should be free.

(*A beat.*)

Do me a favor.

GANYMEDE. Anything.

APOLLO. Easy now.

GANYMEDE. Sorry.

APOLLO. Go back to him. Tell him I can see through his game.

GANYMEDE. Okay...

APOLLO. And I require his lightning. The nectar and ambrosia, they may help sustain him, but this is an insult to me. Without that lightning...without that lightning nothing will bring him back. Tell him if he has any care in his heart, he would know that one mortal isn't a replacement for another.

GANYMEDE. ...That's really going to piss him off. I mean, if I can remember it all.

APOLLO. Remember it. You must tell him that, word for word. Alright?

GANYMEDE. Of course. Okay, yeah. If you say so.

APOLLO. I'm sorry if you bear the brunt of it. But he's always pissed off, isn't he?

GANYMEDE. ...If you order me, I must do it, so...

APOLLO. ...Perhaps, we'll say a prayer first.

GANYMEDE. A prayer?

APOLLO. For your protection. And for the gifts you bring.

GANYMEDE. ...

APOLLO. If you want to join me.

GANYMEDE. You want me to –?

APOLLO. Please. If you do.

> (**GANYMEDE** *goes near him, holds out his hands. Closes his eyes.*)

> (**APOLLO** *mixes the nectar and the ambrosia.*)

> (*He reaches one hand out over* **HYACINTH**'s *body, he holds the mixture in the other.*)

May these gifts strengthen your spirit. And may the mortal who brought them to you be blessed, and no harm brought to him...Take this light, Hyacinth. May this, if nothing else, sustain you.

> (*He rubs the mixture on* **HYACINTH**'s *chest very gently. Then he lays his other hand on him.*)

APOLLO. I will heal you. I promise. I will stop at nothing.

(They come out of the prayer poses.)

APOLLO. Hopefully, that...

GANYMEDE. Hopefully. I don't think anyone knows how much you really care for him. I didn't think any god could care for...truly care for my kind. Makes me sorta question things.

APOLLO. He is philtatos. My treasure.

GANYMEDE. Of his own free will?

APOLLO. Yes. I wanted to make him immortal when he was well. Now, all I want is for him to live the life he was given.

GANYMEDE. I'll tell your father. This time, I'll remember.

APOLLO. Well, he will not harm you for it.

GANYMEDE. He tends to take it easy on me anyway. Because I am mortal. I can't take much. Compared to the gods. I imagine, that's why, to the gods, mortals are the most precious items in the universe. Their vulnerability. It makes them even more desirable...

APOLLO. Irreplaceable.

GANYMEDE. Yes. Precious. Philtatos. But. Anyway. I wish you well. Thank you for your prayer. I'll be praying for you both.

(Thunder crashes. Days pass.)

*(****HYACINTH*** *does not improve.)*

ιη. (Eighteen)

(**APOLLO** *by* **HYACINTH**'s *bedside. A few days later.*)

(**ARTEMIS** *enters.*)

ARTEMIS. Apollo?

APOLLO. ...

ARTEMIS. Have you moved since I was last here?

APOLLO. You have come back.

ARTEMIS. Father sent me.

APOLLO. I thought you left him?

ARTEMIS. I didn't. The idea of war dwindled as the days passed. I lost courage. So I stayed. He didn't want another messenger to tell you. He wanted me to tell you, so. I serve. He is sorry you do not appreciate his gifts, but he cannot lend you his lightning bolt. To restore this man would bring chaos out of order and he...

APOLLO. What?

ARTEMIS. He would not risk bringing chaos for the life of some...silly...

APOLLO. That's clear enough. He couldn't even bother to show up. Say this himself.

ARTEMIS. He insisted it was me who come back. For punishment. I have been too sullen lately and he demands that order return between us.

APOLLO. I see... With no understanding towards you, or me, or our plights...he is just as you said.

ARTEMIS. ...

APOLLO. It is all true...

ARTEMIS. ...

APOLLO. Perhaps the Titans were right. Perhaps they are better for this world. Why should an act of god be anything but an act of love? Zeus deserves to be tossed from the throne!

ARTEMIS. You will challenge him now, too?

APOLLO. I will challenge who I must.

ARTEMIS. In your state?

APOLLO. He tries to convince me of what is real, but I know what's real! I can do this on my own. I never needed anyone.

ARTEMIS. Apollo, there are few gods among us who could heal a broken skull. Zeus included. Even if he did decide to help, I don't think he could. You can think of it that way.

APOLLO. Yeah. Well. Thanks for the message. You did your job. Served your purpose.

ARTEMIS. Fine. Farewell then, and good luck with your revolution.

APOLLO. ...

ARTEMIS. ...

APOLLO. ...At least you got the ending you wanted.

ARTEMIS. ...

APOLLO. The arrogant God...finally punished. Finally brought to the level of the humans whose attention he seeks so much...lower...for he cannot move. He cannot eat. He cannot think. Justice, Artemis, for the god of Justice himself.

ARTEMIS. ...There is no justice here, Apollo.

APOLLO. ...

ARTEMIS. Not when these mortals are always dying for us.

APOLLO. ...

ARTEMIS. Why are they always dying for us?

APOLLO. ...

ARTEMIS. Why are we always killing them?

APOLLO. ...

ARTEMIS. In truth, Apollo. I came back for him... I don't know why.

APOLLO. ...Thank you...

ARTEMIS. I know I told you I'm happy this happened, but I'm not. Not all the time anyway. It changes.

APOLLO. It does?

ARTEMIS. Mostly I find myself just...feeling sorry for you. Feeling my own loss all over again.

APOLLO. So even now I bring you pain?

ARTEMIS. You bring me a pain that reverberates...reminds me of what I used to have. A pain that shoots question after question into the air, like an unhinged prayer... Is this what mortals feel like when they lose someone?

APOLLO. I think so.

ARTEMIS. It's awful.

APOLLO. Yes.

ARTEMIS. It's not fair. It's too much.

APOLLO. What do I do...Artie...

ARTEMIS. ...

APOLLO. My strength runs low. If I let him go...if I leave his side...he'll die...

ARTEMIS. ...Do what you must, but find some peace.

APOLLO. There's no peace in this. Is there any peace for you?

ARTEMIS. ...I don't know. Somehow...there's a bit more of it now.

> (**ARTEMIS** *gently reaches out to her brother and then exits.*)

> (*A beat.*)

APOLLO. Break me, Hyacinth. Break me into a thousand pieces.

It's only then you will have justice. My wrongs have brought this horror on you. You, who were the rarest flower...

So, make me nothing, Hyacinth. Make me into air.

> (**ZEPHYRUS** *enters on the far side of the runway.*)

> (**APOLLO**'*s eyes lock on* **ZEPHYRUS** *as she floats towards him.*)

Why are you here?

ZEPHYRUS. I needed to see. Him. If it would make you happy to strike me down, then –

APOLLO. Please just go.

> (*A moment as she takes in his resignation.*)

ZEPHYRUS. I know my being here causes you pain. But I couldn't seem to silence the thought that...I should finish this. I must bring some peace finally. To him. To you.

APOLLO. You're crazy. Why would I want anything from you?

ZEPHYRUS. I came to tell you I'm sorry.

APOLLO. You came to...

ZEPHYRUS. Apologize.

APOLLO. ...

ZEPHYRUS. I'm sorry that I could not see your love. I'm sorry I hurt a life most precious. I will wish every day that I could change it. Rest with this. Let it bring you satisfaction.

APOLLO. ...

ZEPHYRUS. ...I'll leave now.

APOLLO. Zephyrus...

ZEPHYRUS. ...

APOLLO. We can't change it. Even in all that we can do, all the power we have, I cannot right this wrong.

ZEPHYRUS. ...I have done now what I could. But you are different, Apollo. You can't change all of it, but you can change some things. It is within your power. Transfiguration.

APOLLO. ...

ZEPHYRUS. You can change the body. The soul. Turn it into something new.

APOLLO. Something worthy of him.

ZEPHYRUS. Yes.

APOLLO. And the Titans?

ZEPHYRUS. What of the Titans?

APOLLO. You'll rush back to them. With happy news. He is dead. And another great war begins again.

ZEPHYRUS. I don't blame you for thinking that, but...from what I have learned there is much left to be desired from both sides. I only look to right my wrong. Bring peace. And if you do what I suggest, he will never die. Not really. And there will be no war.

APOLLO. How do I find his soul?

ZEPHYRUS. Only a spirit can find a spirit. Send out yours.

APOLLO. Great. How the fuck do I do that?

ZEPHYRUS. In prayer. Send it out. Seek him.

APOLLO. What if he does not answer? If he hates me...I never told him of my love.

ZEPHYRUS. ...Tell him with this.

(**ZEPHYRUS** *moves back, gives them space.*)

(**APOLLO** *closes his eyes.*)

APOLLO. Hyacinth...

I call to you now. I come bearing gifts. A love to give you in death. A love I never gave in life.

Hyacinth...come to me.

(*The lights shift, we hear* **HYACINTH**'s *voice.*)

Hyacinth...

HYACINTH. (*Voice over.*) Apollo...you're here.

APOLLO. Where have you been?

HYACINTH. (*Voice over.*) Here. I was never far from you.

APOLLO. But you were. Gone. Seeking.

HYACINTH. (*Voice over.*) And I found the truth. It was Zephyrus.

APOLLO. Yes. But it was also me. My sins. An endless list. My love unspoken. I love you.

HYACINTH. (*Voice over.*) I can feel that love. And it has sustained me. From Tartarus. But now...with my body at the brink, my spirit will be sent there.

APOLLO. No. No, Hades will not have you. We will cheat them, Hyacinth. And what's more, I will renew you.

HYACINTH. *(Voice over.)* How?

APOLLO. With our love. Our love will change us both.

HYACINTH. *(Voice over.)* Stretch out your hands, Apollo.

(**APOLLO** *stretches out his hands.*)

Begin with my body

Sit me upright on the ground.

Let my blood seep into the earth.

Let it turn to roots.

Roots that grow down, down to the center of the stadium.

Roots that are so strong they dig into the bedrock

And stop, just above Tartarus.

Turn my waist to green leaves

Lift up my arms and let them sprout petals

Curious, purple petals

With an incredible fragrance.

Make my soul the spine of this flower

Name it after me.

Let me appear at the tail end of winter, marking the first sign of spring.

Let my seeds be carried on the western wind

Let them be taken to the far corners of the planet

Everywhere.

All over Gaia.

Let me come back.

Let me come back every year.

(**APOLLO** *has transformed* **HYACINTH** *into
a flower, which sits on the grounds of the
stadium where his body once was.*)

ZEPHYRUS. He's beautiful.

APOLLO. And he will stand for change. And hope. Forever.

ZEPHYRUS. Forever.

HYACINTH. *(Voice-over.)* Forever.

End of Play